Read with Mummy

Hansel and Gretel

Story retold by Janet Brown
Illustrations by Ken Morton

A long time ago a woodcutter lived with his wife and his two children, Hansel and Gretel. He was so poor that he could not feed his family. So one day he took the children deep into the woods and left them asleep beside a great fire.

"The wild animals will soon find them," he comforted his wife. "It will be better than watching them starve."

Why did the woodcutter leave Hansel and Gretel in the woods?

But clever Hansel said: "Don't worry, Gretel. As we were walking here, I laid a path of white stones. They will shine in the moonlight and lead us home." All night they followed the path of white stones. In the morning they arrived at their house.

Their parents, who had been crying all night, were overjoyed to see them.

How did Hansel and Gretel find their way home again?

But the next day there was still nothing to eat. So the woodcutter took his children back into the woods. "I cannot watch you starve," he said sadly, and he left them asleep beside a great fire.

Clever Hansel said: "Don't worry, Gretel. As we were walking here, I laid a path of white bread. It will shine in the moonlight and lead us home."

But all day long the birds had been pecking at the bread-path. By evening there was nothing left – and Hansel and Gretel were lost in the woods.

They lay down in the leaves to wait for morning.

What happened to Hansel's path of white bread?

The next day Hansel and Gretel walked for miles. They saw trees and grass and birds and sky – but they could not find their way home. They were cold and hungry.

Suddenly, they came upon a gingerbread house. The roof was made of icing, the windows were spun sugar and the door was marshmallow.

The children fell on the house and stuffed their mouths full of sweet things.

What was the house in the woods made of?

An old lady appeared. "Welcome, children!" she said. "Why don't you come inside and eat properly?"

Inside she gave them hot chocolate with cream and pancakes with strawberries. Then she tucked them up in bed. "Rest for a while, my dears," she told them.

The children did not know that the old lady was a witch in disguise – a witch who ate little children!

Who was the old lady, underneath her disguise?

When the children awoke, the witch gave them breakfast. Then she pushed Hansel into a big cage and locked him in! "You will stay there until you have grown fat!" she cackled. "And then I will eat you!"

Every day the witch said to Hansel: "Stick out your finger so I can see how fat you are!" Every day Hansel stuck a thin piece of wood through the bars.

"Feed him more food!" screeched the witch. So poor Gretel had to feed him more food, and Hansel grew fatter and fatter.

How did Hansel fool the witch into thinking he was still thin?

Finally the witch was tired of waiting. She lit the oven. Then she said to Gretel: "Climb into the oven, child, and tell me if it is hot enough."

"How will I know if it is hot enough?" asked Gretel.

"Silly girl! I will do it myself," said the witch. She climbed into the oven – and Gretel slammed the oven-door shut!

Then she ran to let Hansel out of the cage.

Why did the witch climb into the oven?

The children hugged each other and cried for joy. They filled their pockets with gold from the witch's treasure chest, and food for the journey. Then they ran away from the gingerbread house.

When the children escaped from the gingerbread house,
what did they take with them?

The children finally found their way home. Their parents, who were ill and starving by this time, came out to greet them. When they saw how fat Hansel was, they were amazed. And when they saw the food and the gold, they were even *more* amazed!

So the woodcutter and his wife were never hungry again. And Hansel and Gretel lived to be very old and very fat, with children of their own.

Why were the woodcutter and his wife amazed when they saw Hansel and Gretel?

On a piece of paper practise writing these words.
Can you find them again in the story?

lost in the woods

witch

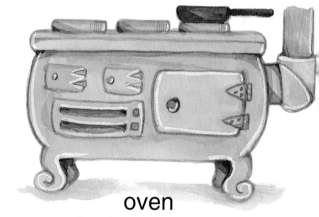

oven

bucket

jewels